Dear Parents and Educators,

Welcome to Penguin Young Readers! As parents and educators, you know that each child develops at his or her own pace—in terms of speech, critical thinking, and, of course, reading. Penguin Young Readers recognizes this fact. As a result, each Penguin Young Readers book is assigned a traditional easy-to-read level (1–4) as well as a Guided Reading Level (A–P). Both of these systems will help you choose the right book for your child. Please refer to the back of each book for specific leveling information. Penguin Young Readers features esteemed authors and illustrators, stories about favorite characters, fascinating nonfiction, and more!

Dick and Jane: Jump and Run

LEVEL **1**

GUIDED
READING
LEVEL **D**

This book is perfect for an **Emergent Reader** who:
• can read in a left-to-right and top-to-bottom progression;
• can recognize some beginning and ending letter sounds;
• can use picture clues to help tell the story; and
• can understand the basic plot and sequence of simple stories.

Here are some **activities** you can do during and after reading this book:
• Sight Words: Sight words are frequently used words that readers must know just by looking at them. These words are not "sounded out" or "decoded"; rather they are known instantly, on sight. Knowing these words helps children develop into efficient readers. As you read the story, have the child point out the sight words listed below.

and	come	is	play	see
big	down	little	run	work
can	help	look	said	you

• On a separate piece of paper, work with the child to write a new sentence for each of the words listed in the chart.

Remember, sharing the love of reading with a child is the best gift you can give!

—Bonnie Bader, EdM, and Katie Carella, EdM
   Penguin Young Readers program

*Penguin Young Readers are leveled by independent reviewers applying the standards developed by Irene Fountas and Gay Su Pinnell in *Matching Books to Readers: Using Leveled Books in Guided Reading*, Heinemann, 1999.

PENGUIN YOUNG READERS
Published by the Penguin Group
Penguin Group (USA) LLC
375 Hudson Street
New York, New York 10014, USA

USA | Canada | UK | Ireland | Australia | New Zealand | India | South Africa | China

penguin.com
A Penguin Random House Company

Library of Congress Control Number: 2003016956

ISBN 978-0-448-43402-5   20

Dick and Jane
Jump and Run

Penguin Young Readers
An Imprint of Penguin Group (USA) Inc.

Contents

Chapter 1
Puff

Jump, Puff.

Jump, jump, jump.

Jump, Puff, jump.

Run, Puff.

Run, Puff, run.

Run, run, run.

Jump, jump, jump.

Oh, Puff.

Oh, oh, oh.

Funny, funny Puff.

Chapter 2
Spot

Come, come.

Come, Spot, come.

Run, run, run.

Jump, Spot.

Jump, jump.

Jump, Spot, jump.

Oh, Spot.

Oh, oh, oh.

Funny, funny Spot.

Chapter 3
Jump and Play

Sally said, "Oh, look.

Mother can jump.

Mother can jump and play."

Dick said, "Jump, Father.

You can jump.

You can jump and play."

"Look, Mother," said Sally.

"See Father jump.

See Father jump and play.

Big, big Father is funny."

Jane said, "Oh, Father.

You can not jump and play.

Spot can not jump and play."

Dick said, "Oh, see Puff.

Puff can jump.

Puff can jump and play."

Chapter 4
Run and Help

Run, Jane.

Help Mother.

Run, Jane, run.

Help Mother work.

Come, Sally, come.

Come and help.

Come and help Mother.

Run, run, run.

Look, Sally, look.

See Spot work.

Funny, funny Spot.

Oh, oh, oh.

Spot can help Mother.

Chapter 5
See Puff Jump

Look, Dick.

See Puff jump.

Oh, look.

Look and see.

See Puff jump and play.

Come, Jane, come.

Come and see Puff.

See Puff jump and run.

See funny, little Puff.

Oh, oh, oh.

See little Puff run.

Oh, see Puff.

Funny, little Puff.

Chapter 6
Spot and Tim and Puff

Spot can jump.

Little Puff can jump.

Look, Tim, look.

See Spot and Puff play.

Look, Tim.

See Sally jump.

See Sally jump down.

Down, down, down.

Sally can jump and play.

Oh, Puff.

See funny, little Tim.

See Tim jump down.

Down, down, down.

Tim can jump and play.

Chapter 7
Oh, See

Look, Sally, look.

Look down.

Look down, Sally.

Look down, down, down.

Look up, Sally.

Look up, up, up.

Run, Sally, run.

Run and jump.

Run and jump up.

Look, Jane.

Look and see.

Oh, see.

See funny, funny Sally.